ANIMALS FROM MY WINDOW

Story by **Regina Gershman**

Illustrated by **E. Jackie Brown**

AuthorHouse™
1663 Liberty Drive
Bloomington, IN 47403
www.authorhouse.com
Phone: 1-800-839-8640

First published by AuthorHouse 9/9/2011

ISBN: 978-1-4634-2094-9 (sc)

Library of Congress Control Number: 2011910760

authorHOUSE®

TABLE OF CONTENTS

ANIMALS FROM MY WINDOW

Every morning as I wake up and look out the window I see our animals. We have so many different animals on the farm. We have chickens, ducks, turkeys, pigs, cows, horses, dogs and cats.

Let's talk about all of them...

LET'S TALK ABOUT CHICKENS

A female chicken is called a *Hen* and a male chicken is called a *Rooster.*

A hen makes eggs for children to eat. Did you know that an average hen could lay from 60 – 120 eggs a year? These eggs must be picked up at least once a day; otherwise they will not be fresh. Chickens eat mostly grain, seeds and whatever they can find in the grass.

Chickens can bite people, usually by a little peck on a hand, if they think someone is trying to take their eggs away.

The sound a CHICKEN makes is CLUCK...CLUCK.... CLUCK....

LET'S TALK ABOUT DUCKS

Ducks need to live near clean water. Ducks are usually kept in small groups. In the spring ducks lay eggs and these eggs are picked up by farmers and put in the incubator until they hatch. The male duck is called a *Drake* and the baby ducks are called *Ducklings*.

The ducks love to eat cereal grain, fishmeal, grass and green vegetables.

The sound DUCKS make is QUACK...QUACK... QUACK...

LET'S TALK ABOUT TURKEYS

Did you know that even though turkeys have wings, they seldom fly? This is because most domestic turkeys are so heavy they are unable to fly.

There are different kinds of turkeys; there are Slate turkeys, which have grayish brown spots on the tail. There are white turkeys with red heads and black turkeys with red heads.

The adult male turkey is called *Tom* and the adult female turkey is called a *Hen*. In mature males, the feathers of the train or tail are all the same length, forming a circular fan when spread. Very young turkeys are called *Poults* and a young male turkey is called *Jake*. They can be identified by the shape of their "tail". In Jakes, the feathers near the edges are shorter. Turkeys eat mostly grain.

The sound TURKEYS make is GOBBLE... GOBBLE... GOBBLE.

LET'S TALK ABOUT PIGS

I bet you think that pigs are dirty animals, but no, they are not. They are very clean animals. Not all pigs are pink in color; some are black or brown and kind of reddish, and have long drooping ears. The female pig is called a *Sow* and the male pig is called a *Boar.* Baby pigs are called P*iglets.* There are usually 8 to 10 little piglets in a large family.

Piglets love to run around the pen. Pigs love to eat leftovers such as corn, potatoes, and any sort of cereals, and plants. Pigs like to roll in the mud to cool off. Pigs usually grunt when communicating with each other.

LET'S TALK ABOUT COWS

Cows are also very important animals in our everyday life. Without cows we wouldn't have fresh milk, butter, yogurt and other dairy products.

There are different breeds of cows – dairy cows that are black and white or red and white are called *Holstein* cows. Holstein cows are big farm cows. These cows need to be milked two to three times per day. Dairy cows are kept indoors most of the time. There is also a smaller breed of cows called *Jersey* cows that are light yellowish in color with white markings.

The sound COWS make is MOO... MOO... MOO...

LET'S TALK ABOUT HORSES

It is very important to take good care of a horse. A horse must be washed, groomed and fed everyday. They eat mostly hay and grass, also love carrots and apples. During spring and summer, horses munch on the grass all day long. The adult female horse is called a *Mare* and the adult male horse is called a *Stallion*. A young female horse, less than four years old, is called a *Filly*. Baby horses are called *Foals* and young horses are called *Colts*.

The sound HORSES make is NEIGH... NEIGH... NEIGH...

LET'S TALK ABOUT DOGS

When puppies are born their eyes are closed. They are completely dependent on their mother to give them milk and wash them. They like to keep warm, so they snuggle to their brothers and sisters.

Dogs must be kept healthy and happy so they have a long and active life. A dog needs to be trained and exercised every day for it to be a good farm dog.

The sound DOGS make is WOOF... WOOF.... WOOF...

LET'S TALK ABOUT CATS

The cats are very affectionate and cuddly animals that get along well with everyone on the farm. They like lying around in the sun, warming their tummies. When they are hungry they eat cat food, but there are times when they beg for fresh milk. Their job is hunting mice on the farm. They are also great in raising kittens; mother cats teach their young how to catch mice. A good cat is an asset to any farm!

The sound CATS make is MEOW... MEOW.... MEOW....

Regina Gershman is an author of children's picture books, fiction and science fiction, including Animals From My Window, which is Regina's second book and The Power of The Magic Word. This book has received Honorable Mention Award in the "Children's Story Writing" from Achieve The Dream.

Born in Kiev, Ukraine, she moved with her parents to Canada when she was 11-years-old. Regina lives in Edmonton, Alberta with her beloved cat, Frisky, and her two sons. She as a business and image consultant. Regina has received a degree from Institute of Children's Literatrure: Writing for Children and Teenagers in 1993. Regina Gershman is a member of Canadian Society of Children's Authors, Illustrators and Performers (CANSCAIP) and Alberta Society of Artists.

CPSIA information can be obtained
at www.ICGtesting.com
Printed in the USA
249292LV00002B